This book belongs to

....

Fun ideas for the Storyteller

Mama Tiger, Baba Tiger is a warm family story, perfect for sharing. Young children will identify with this story's theme of wanting to be grown-up.

Read on to find out how to get the most fun out of this story.

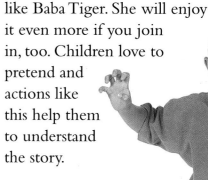

Be a BIG tiger

Ask your child to roar and pounce like a tiger, and to stand on tiptoe to be BIG like Baba Tiger. She will enjoy it even more if you join in, too. Children love to pretend and actions like this help them to understand the story.

Say it like Baba

Read and point to the title, then let your child turn the pages. Encourage him to share the reading, beginning with repeated lines, such as *"Baba, are you on your own?"* When your child is ready, he can say Baba Tiger's lines. Don't worry if his version doesn't quite match the text.

Out and about

Encourage your child to talk about growing up and keeping safe.
Baba Tiger starts out very confident, but then becomes afraid.
Why? Ask your child what he would do if he were Baba Tiger.
Let him know that his ideas are
important to you. This
story calls for a good
cuddle at the end!

Roar
Roar!

Look closely – can you see Mama Tiger?

Look closely at the pictures to see what Mama Tiger is doing while
Baba walks home. Look at Baba Tiger's face to find out how
he feels. Point out the scenery and ask your child to
imagine living in the jungle. Would he like to have lots
of animal friends?

Have a good time and enjoy
the adventure of the story!

Wendy Cooling
Reading Consultant

To Lucie - Juli and Graham

Dorling  Kindersley

LONDON, NEW YORK, SYDNEY, DELHI, PARIS
MUNICH and JOHANNESBURG

Produced by Leapfrog
First published in Great Britain in 2001
by Dorling Kindersley Limited,
9 Henrietta Street, London WC2E 8PS

2 4 6 8 10 9 7 5 3 1
Text copyright © 2001 Juli Mahr
Illustrations copyright © 2001 Graham Percy
The author's and illustrator's moral rights have been asserted.

A CIP catalogue record for this book is available from the British Library.
ISBN 0-7513-7218-8
Colour reproduction by Dot Gradations, UK
Printed by Wing King Tong in China

Acknowledgements:
Reading Consultant: Wendy Cooling **Activities Advisor:** Lianna Hodson
Photographer: Steve Gorton **Models:** Georgia Lilley, Samuel Lilley, Brian Lilley, Sharon Warren

see our complete
catalogue at
www.dk.com

Mama Tiger, Baba Tiger

Juli Mahr   Illustrated by Graham Percy

A Dorling Kindersley Book

Mama Tiger and Baba Tiger were on their way home from their afternoon swim.
"Mama Tiger," asked Baba Tiger, "now that I'm almost grown, can I walk home on my own?"

"Well," said Mama Tiger, "you're still very small."

"But I'm very Big!"
said Baba Tiger.
"I can already do
a Big Tiger hop...

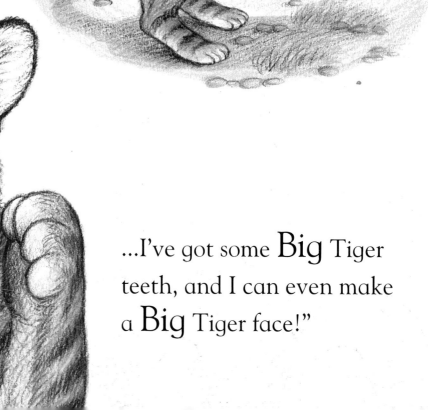

...I've got some Big Tiger
teeth, and I can even make
a Big Tiger face!"

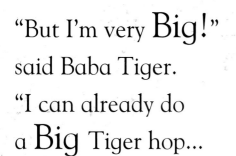

"Alright, dear" chuckled Mama Tiger, "but remember, Baba, if you get into trouble roar like a Big Tiger and I'll come to get you."

Now, Baba knew the way home well and it wasn't long before he came to the great lake. Baba waved and showed off to his friends.

"This is easy," thought the happiest
little Big Tiger there ever was.
And so he continued, feeling
prouder with each step.

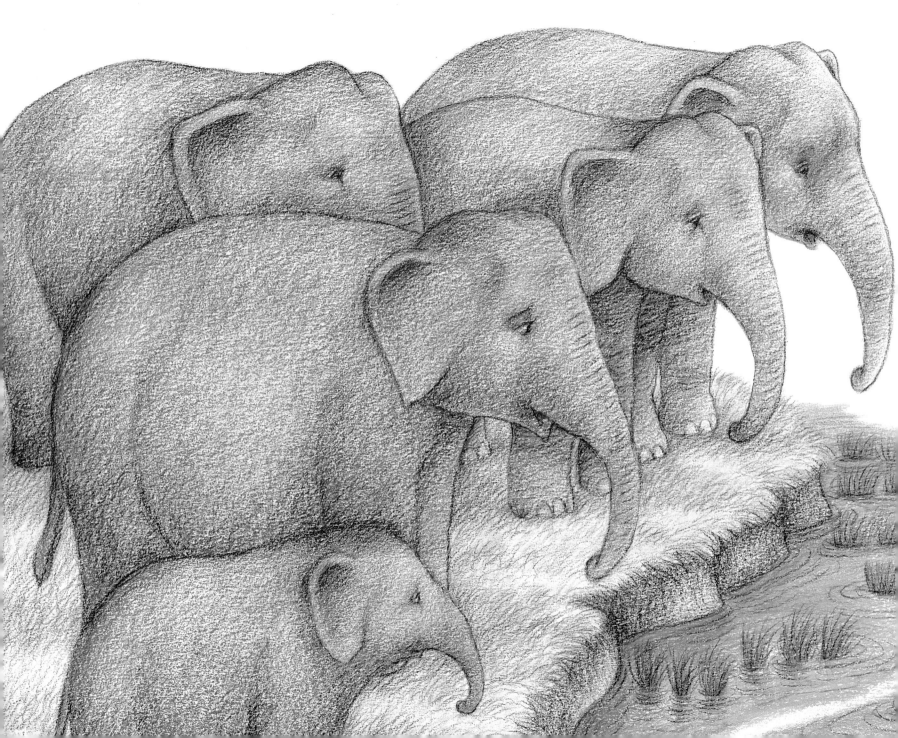

Soon Baba arrived at the marshes where he met some
elephant friends.

"Baba," said Mama Elephant, "are you on your own?"

"Oh yes," said Baba holding his head high,

"because I'm a Big Tiger now...see!"

Baba leapt into the lake and splashed,

as he'd seen Big Tigers do.

Then Baba set off through the
marshes and into the grasslands.
There he bumped into
Old Grandfather Rhino,
stamping his foot into
the ground.
"Baba," said the rhino,
"are you on your own?"

"Oh yes," said Baba holding his head higher,
"because I'm a Big Tiger now...see!"
Baba stuck his tail in the air and swished it
from side to side as he'd seen Big Tigers do.

Baba continued into the great plain. His paws were a little sore but he didn't want to stop. And it wasn't long before he came across his friends the deer.

"Baba," said King Deer, "are you on your own?"

"Oh yes," said Baba holding his head so high that he could no longer see where he was going, "because I'm a Big Tiger now...see!" Baba jumped up and pointed all his toes as he'd seen Big Tigers do.

And so Baba continued across the plain and into the jungle.
He was tired now but he kept going until he came across a group
of monkeys, swinging in the trees. He didn't know any of them.
"Hey little tiger," called out a scruffy young monkey,
"what are you doing on your own?"
"I'm a Big Tiger," said Baba, feeling a little smaller, "and...

"A tough guy, eh?" whistled another monkey.
"Well show us – climb this tree."

Baba lifted his tired head.
He felt sore right up to
his shoulders.
"Alright," he gulped as he
took a few steps back and
ran for the tree.

He only just made it.

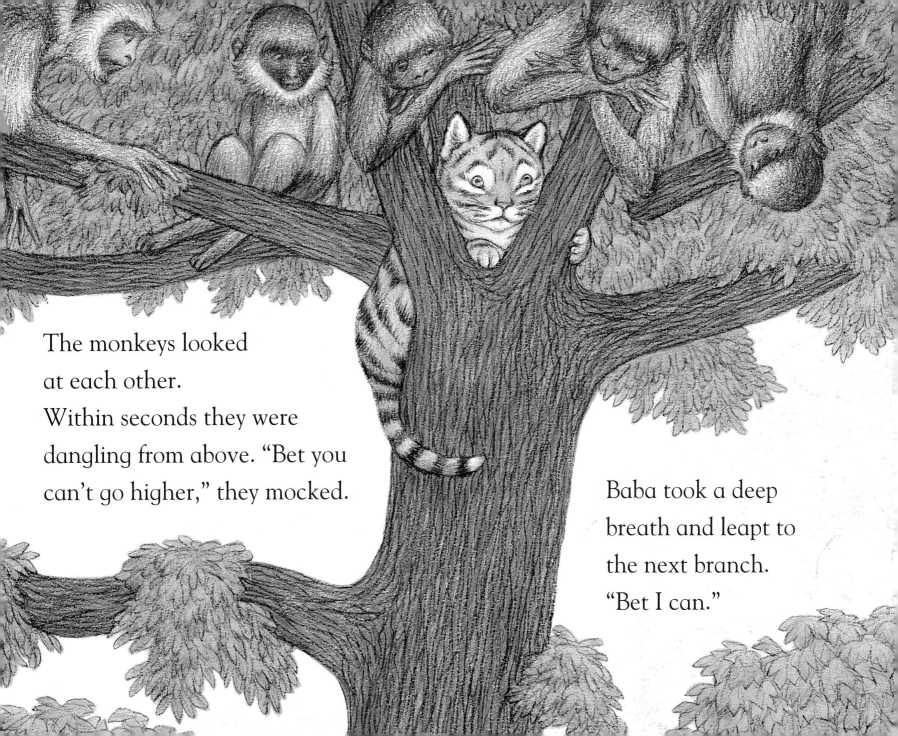

The monkeys looked
at each other.
Within seconds they were
dangling from above. "Bet you
can't go higher," they mocked.

Baba took a deep
breath and leapt to
the next branch.
"Bet I can."

But before Baba could even look up, the monkeys had disappeared. "Let's see you get down again!" they screeched as they ran away.

Baba looked at the ground. It was a long way down. He tried to think **Big** Tiger thoughts, but he'd never seen a tiger climb down from so high.

Baba looked out at
the dark jungle.
All he wanted was for
Mama to look after him.
Baba sniffled and
tried not to cry.

Then, just as Baba was about to
give up hope, he remembered
something – the **Big** Tiger Roar.
With the last of his strength,
he let out the tiniest big roar
there ever was.

Mama was beside him in an instant then. She picked him up as gently as she could and took him down.

"There," said Mama, "all safe."

"Perhaps I'm not so big after all,"
said Baba, his eyelids heavy with sleep.
"Can I be small a little while longer?"

"Of course you can, my little big tiger,"
whispered Mama.
And she picked him up and carried him
the rest of the way home.

Activities to Enjoy

If you've enjoyed this story, you might like to try some of these simple, fun activities with your child.

B is for "Baba"

Show your child the words *Baba* and *BIG* in the story. Say the words, stressing the *B* sound. Draw a large *B* on a piece of paper. (You may want to concentrate on capital *B* to avoid confusion.) Take your child's finger and trace the shape of the letter. She may also want to try drawing over the letter with your help.

Baba Tiger

Ball

Boat

Butterfly

Go on a *B* hunt!

Find things around the house that begin with the letter *B*. Next draw all the things you have found on your *B* hunt. Put Baba Tiger at the top of your list!

Boy

Ball

Balloon

Baba

Bucket

Bricks

Bananas

Boots

Places you might pass on the way to the library:

Home   **Playground**   **Shops**   **Park**   **Library**

Places you pass

Baba Tiger passes many places on his way home. Point out special places that you and your child pass on familiar journeys. Ask your child to draw a picture of each place. Then put the pictures in order to make a simple line map.

Roar! Be a stripey tiger

Use face paints or make-up to make your child look like a tiger. This is a good chance to act out the story.

1. Paint white stripes all around the face, leaving gaps as shown. Paint the eyelids and the area above the eyes white, feathering upwards.

3. Add black spots for the tiger muzzle, and you're ready to roar!

2. Add black and orange stripes in between the white ones. Paint the tip of the nose pink, and outline the lips in black.

Roar Roar!

Other Share-a-Story titles to collect:

Not Now Mrs Wolf! by Shen Roddie, illustrated by Selina Young

Nigel's Numberless World by Lucy Coats, illustrated by Neal Layton

Are You Spring? by Caroline Pitcher, illustrated by Cliff Wright

The Caterpillar That Roared by Michael Lawrence,
illustrated by Alison Bartlett

Where's Bitesize? by Ian Whybrow,
illustrated by Penny Dann

Clara and Buster Go Moondancing by Dyan Sheldon,
illustrated by Caroline Anstey

I Like Me by Laurence Anholt, illustrated by Adriano Gon